©2017 Moose. Cutie Cars™ logos, names and characters are licensed trademarks of Moose Enterprise (INT) Pty Ltd. All rights reserved. All rights reserved. Published by Scholastic Inc., *Publishers since 1920.* SCHOLASTIC and associated logos are trademarks and/or registered trademarks of Scholastic Inc.

The publisher does not have any control over and does not assume any responsibility for author or third-party websites or their content.

No part of this publication may be reproduced, stored in a retrieval system, or transmitted in any form or by any means, electronic, mechanical, photocopying, recording, or otherwise, without written permission of the publisher. For information regarding permission, write to Scholastic Inc., Attention: Permissions Department, 557 Broadway, New York, NY 10012.

This book is a work of fiction. Names, characters, places, and incidents are either the product of the author's imagination or are used fictitiously, and any resemblance to actual persons, living or dead, business establishments, events, or locales is entirely coincidental.

ISBN 978-1-338-22528-0

10 9 8 7 6 5 4 3 2 1   17 18 19 20 21

Printed in the U.S.A.   40

First printing 2017 • Book design by Erin McMahon

SCHOLASTIC INC.

Buckle up and meet the Cutie Cars, the most adorable things on four wheels. Often seen zooming around Shopville, these speedy sweeties are full of fun!

Lollipop Soft Top

Model: Convertible Cutie

Features: Fueled by candy to keep go-go-going

Likes: The sweet side of life

Dislikes: Having sticky seats from sticky sweets

Cupcake Cruiser

Model: Buggy Buddy

Features: Baked for a wheely sweet ride

Likes: Picnics in the park—they're the cherry best!

Dislikes: When her windshield gets frosty

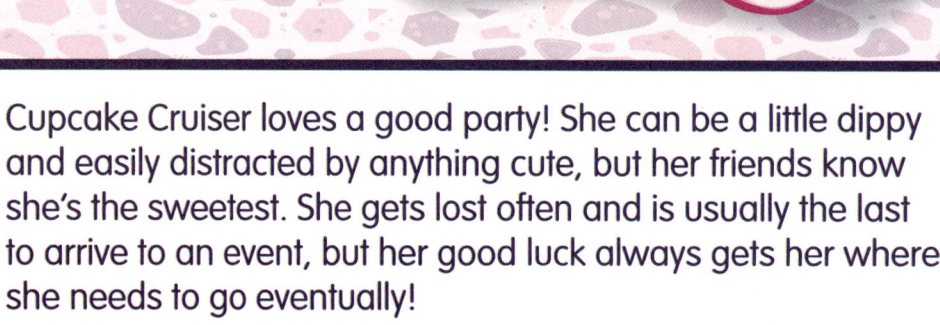

Cupcake Cruiser loves a good party! She can be a little dippy and easily distracted by anything cute, but her friends know she's the sweetest. She gets lost often and is usually the last to arrive to an event, but her good luck always gets her where she needs to go eventually!

Popcorn Moviegoer

Model: Fun Food Van

Features: A warm and buttery interior

Likes: Poppin' tunes on the radio

Dislikes: Scary movies—they make him spill his popcorn.

Donut Express

Model: Fun Food Van

Features: A hole lot of sweet and tasteful styling

Likes: Rolling up to parties and sprinkling her friends with treats

Dislikes: Sharp corners

Constantly on the go, this Cutie Car is always running on a sugar buzz! Filled with positive thoughts, she makes her way through the day without a worry in the world. No matter what, everything always seems to fall into place for her.

Sundae Scooter

Model: Buggy Buddy

Features: Cool looks make for a super chill ride!

Likes: Sharing a sundae drive with friends

Dislikes: When it's sprinkling outside

Peely Apple Wheels

Model: Buggy Buddy

Features: Crisp handling without using much juice

Likes: Getting to the core of matters

Dislikes: Bumpy rides that bruise her wheels

A bit of a teacher's pet, Peely Apple Wheels is always telling other Cutie Cars to follow the rules of the road. She cares about the environment and is always thinking of new ways to save the world—she truly believes in going green!

Traveling Taco

Model: Fun Food Van

Features: Tacos with a taste you'll want to chase

Likes: Salsa dancing with her amigos

Dislikes: Shelling out lots of cash to park

Motor Melon is a natural leader. She is always the first to try something new and loves taking the Cutie Cars on "the road less traveled." Confident and friendly, she greets her friends with a wheely high five or a "Bumper Bump!"

Motor Melon

Model: Convertible Cutie
Features: Runs on water from a big fuel tank
Likes: Breezy summer drives go a long way on a hot day!
Dislikes: Gray, drizzling skies

Frozen Yocart

Model: Speedy SUV

Features: A very cool interior and smooth finish

Likes: Whipping up a treat for friends to eat

Dislikes: Getting lost and swirling around in circles

Ice Cream Dream Car

Model: Fun Food Van

Features: A set of cool wheels to whip around town

Likes: Serving up sweet tricks

Dislikes: Traffic cones—they're definitely not as good as waffle cones!

Jelly Bean Machine

Model: Fun Food Van

Features: A one-stop jelly bean shop

Likes: Adding a bit of color wherever she goes

Dislikes: Surprise flavors

Choc Chip Racer

Model: Convertible Cutie

Features: Clever and high-tech, she's one smart cookie!

Likes: Chipping in to help friends

Dislikes: Rocky roads—they make her crumble.

Choc Chip Racer is always challenging others to a race. She loves to show off her driving skills and dunk right into risky tricks—but she's also great at looking out for her friends.

Zoomy Noodles

Model: Speedy SUV

Features: A lot of space that holds oodles of noodles

Likes: Handling the hard delivery jobs

Dislikes: Soup-er steep hills

Jelly Joyride

Model: Buggy Buddy

Features: Soft, bouncy seats and airbags

Likes: Clear visibility

Dislikes: Feeling wobbly on her wheels around winding roads

Milk Moover is ready to offer motherly advice to the other Cutie Cars 24/7. She's always there to comfort any cars who may have a scratch or dent after a little accident. Super reliable, Milk Moover delivers on every promise she makes!

Milk Moover

Model: Speedy SUV

Features: A smooth moover, even in those worst of milkshakes

Likes: Dairy-ing adventures

Dislikes: Spilt milk in the road

Wheely Wishes

Model: Speedy SUV

Features: Everything you've wished for in a car

Likes: To be the life of the party

Dislikes: When her headlights burn out

Royal Roadster

LIMITED EDITION

Model: Convertible Cutie
Features: You will feel like a princess in this royal ride!
Likes: Waving to her admirers as she drives by
Dislikes: When dirt from the roads covers her sparkles

Sneaky Speedster

Model: Convertible Cutie
Features: This car has lots of sole!
Likes: Going fast
Dislikes: Getting tied up in traffic

LIMITED EDITION

Flashy Fashionista

Model: Buggy Buddy

Features: A luxurious luggage compartment

Likes: Carrying on with her best friends

Dislikes: When her clutch is broken

Flashy Fashionista loves to be seen parked in all the best streets in town. Her windows are always rolled down with the radio volume turned up, and she stops to pose at every speed camera she sees. Her favorite pastime is getting a car wash and detail to make sure she always looks her best!